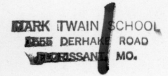

Mr. Sipple and the

by Jan Slepian and Ann Seidler

Follett Publishing Company   Chicago

Naughty Princess

illustrated by Richard E. Martin

MISTER Sipple hurried as fast as an old seal can hurry. He wished he had a fat fish in his stomach because he was hungry. He wished the ball he carried on his nose weren't so heavy because he was tired. He wished his fur were thicker because he was cold. Even his red scarf didn't seem warm enough. But he knew that the young seals in the nearby kingdom were waiting for him to sing and do his tricks, so he didn't stop to rest or eat.

4

In the distance he could see the towers of the snow castle where King Seal lived with his little daughter, Princess Silverskin. Mr. Sipple wondered if she were waiting for him too. Three ice hills to the left, one snow slide to the right, and he was with his friends at last.

"Mithter Thipple, your thinging theal, ith here!" he shouted to a group of young seals. He flipped the ball from his nose to his tongue and back again, expecting the usual laughter.

No one laughed. "Hello, Mr. Sipple," they greeted him sadly. Some were even crying little ice tears onto the snow.

"Why tho thad, my little oneth?" he asked, tossing the
ball with his strong tongue.

"S-s-sad," only one little voice corrected.

"That'th what I thaid . . . *thad*. Well, I'll thoon
fikth your thadneth." And he started to spin the ball
around on his nose and sing:

>Thing a thong of thickthpenth.
>A pocket full of fish.

"Aw, that's 'S-s-sing a S-s-song of S-s-sixpence'," said one small seal. "We don't want to hear that song today. We need help."

"Yes! Yes! That's what we need," they all clamored. "Oh, if you only could. . . . It's Princess Silverskin, Mr. Sipple!"

"Printheth Thilverthkin? What happened?" he asked.

"She won't go to sleep, and she has been so cross and naughty! Oooh, what bad things she does! And now she has locked herself up in one of the tall towers of the snow castle and won't come out."

Kind Mr. Sipple wanted to help. Perhaps he could sing her to sleep. . . . Suddenly he remembered a very pretty song about sunsets and ice.

"I know how to put her to thleep!" he cried.

"Oh, Mr. Sipple, whatever you do, she'll know you and laugh," said the seals.

"Maybe not. Jutht wait," he said mysteriously. "Come along, everyone."

So they all set out for the castle.

What they had heard about the princess was all too true. She had indeed thrown the whole kingdom into an uproar with her naughty tricks.

The princess' worried father, the king, had tried everything he could think of to get her to sleep. The people of the kingdom had tried everything they could think of to get her to sleep. Nothing had worked. She had just become crosser and naughtier.

The king had brought her warm milk in her favorite red bowl, but she had grabbed the bowl from his hands and tossed the milk and the bowl out the window. The bowl had landed upside down with a great splash of milk on the head of a fat old seal who was passing by. Of course the milk had frozen right away so that it looked as if the seal had white hair and a long white beard.

"It's Santa Claus! Santa Claus!" the little seals who were on their way home from school had shouted. So the king had given presents to all those little seals to keep them happy. All because Princess Silverskin wouldn't sleep.

The poor king also had the finest, softest bird feathers sewn onto the princess' favorite blanket. He had tucked her into her little bed, and had all the seals of the court crowd into her room to help put her to sleep. Over and over they had said as softly as they could, "Ssssssleeeep, sssssssleeeep, sssssssssleeeeep," until, one by one, all the court seals had fallen asleep.

Only the princess had stayed wide awake! Then she had pulled off all the soft bird feathers from the blanket and put a feather on the nose of each of the sleeping seals. They had all awakened sneezing, *"Kerchoo! Kerchoo!"* The feathers had blown every which way, and the room had looked as if a snow storm had struck it. All because Princess Silverskin wouldn't sleep.

And now she had locked herself up in one of the tall towers of the snow castle and wouldn't come out.

"Quickly, quickly," Mr. Sipple urged the young seals. And soon they were at the foot of the tower.

The old singer put down his trick ball.

"Here ith thomebody to thing you a thleep thong," he called, covering part of his face with his red scarf so that the princess wouldn't know him. As the pretty little princess leaned out of the window at the top of the tower, Mr. Sipple sang in his best voice:

> Thunthetth are red, ithe ith blue.
> Prin. . . .

Splat! Before he had time to finish, the princess threw a snowball right on his head.

"I know you, Mr. Sipple," she laughed. "You can't fool me."

Mr. Sipple wiped the snow from his head and turned sadly away. His little friends whispered together. One little fellow pulled at him and said, "Don't give up yet. We'll dress you up. Then the princess won't know who you are and you can sing her to sleep."

So the young seals dressed Mr. Sipple up as Granddaddy Walrus. They put two icicles in his mouth for tusks and powdered him all over with snow. With a stick for a cane, he hobbled back to the snow tower.

"Old Granddaddy Walruth ith here to thing you a thleep thong, dear Printheth," Mr. Sipple called. He started to sing:

> Thunthetth are red, ithe. . . .

Squish! Another snowball fell on his head and the icicles popped out of his mouth.

"I still know you, Mr. Sipple," giggled the princess.

"What can I do?" Mr. Sipple moaned. She always knew him!

"I know," said one smart little fellow. "It's the way you sing. If you could sing *sssssun-ssssetsss* and *i-ssss* she wouldn't know who you were."

"Yes," said another. "Ssss—like wind whistling around the icebergs. Sssssssssss!"

"Or like ice squeaking under your flippers—sssssssssss," said still another seal.

Mr. Sipple nodded his head. "You're right. I'll try it!"

This time the seals put reindeer horns on Mr. Sipple's head and threw an old reindeer skin around him. With the horns slipping over one eye, Mr. Sipple went back to the tower. He thought of the wind whistling: s-s-s-s-s-s-s. He thought of ice squeaking: s-s-s-s-s-s. But try as he might, something was still wrong:

Th-th-thunthetth are red. . . .

This time a whole rain of snowballs came down on him. His horns were knocked off as he dodged and ducked. His head was busy. His flippers were busy. Even his strong trick tongue was busy bouncing the snowballs off. Soon his tongue became so cold that the weary old singer had to warm it in his mouth behind his teeth.

"Sssssstop! Sssssstop, I sssay!" he called, his cold tongue still hiding behind his teeth.

"That's it! That's the *sssss* of the wind and the *sssss* of the ice! Sing, Mr. Sipple! Sing!" begged his little seal friends.

And so Mr. Sipple sang his song. Softly and sweetly it rose in the clear, cold air, reaching the ears of the princess like a gentle kiss.

S-S-S-Sunsets are red, ice is blue.
Princess Silverskin, goodnight to you.

Over and over, Mr. Sipple sang his lullabye while the princess' head drooped, her eyes closed, and at last she slept. She slept and slept and slept, even before she was tucked into bed. She slept and slept and slept while the kingdom rejoiced and the grateful king rewarded Mr. Sipple with half the kingdom and all the fish he could eat.

28

No longer did Mr. Sipple wander from kingdom to kingdom. Instead he stayed in his own to rest and enjoy his friends.

Every night he sang the little princess to sleep, and she was never so naughty again.

THE LISTEN-HEAR BOOKS

The Listen-Hear books provide teachers and parents with an entertaining and simple method of speech improvement for children in kindergarten and the early primary grades. The books also provide imaginative and enjoyable stories.

The books were written especially for the child who would benefit from ear training in order to improve his auditory discrimination. He is a child with normal hearing whose speech contains a common childhood error—the child who says *wed*, for instance, and thinks he is saying *red*. The stories and illustrations are so imaginative, however, that all children enjoy them. The stories also help all children develop good speaking habits, which in turn help develop good reading habits.

The books are ideal for read-aloud time. The *Teacher's Guide* for the set of six books provides instructions for games that the children can play after they have heard each story. The games give children practice in listening, hearing, and making the correct sounds.

Each book deals with one sound that many children find difficult to make:

> The Roaring Dragon of Redrose—for the sound of *R*
> Magic Arthur and the Giant—for the sound of *Th*
> Mr. Sipple and the Naughty Princess—for the sound of *S*
> The Cock Who Couldn't Crow—for the sound of *K*
> Alfie and the Dream Machine—for the sound of *F*
> Lester and the Sea Monster—for the sound of *L*

The authors, Jan Slepian and Ann Seidler, have each had more than ten years experience in speech therapy.

Mrs. Slepian has been a speech therapist at the Language Clinic at Massachusetts General Hospital in Boston and the National Hospital for Speech Disorders in New York.

Mrs. Seidler has been a speech therapist at the National Hospital for Speech Disorders in New York and speech consultant for the public schools of Cedar Grove, New Jersey.